THE ADVENTURES OF
ROBIN HOOD

THE ADVENTURES OF
ROBIN HOOD

Retold by Russell Punter

Illustrated by Matteo Pincelli

Series editors:
Lesley Sims and Jane Chisholm

Consultant: Mike Collins

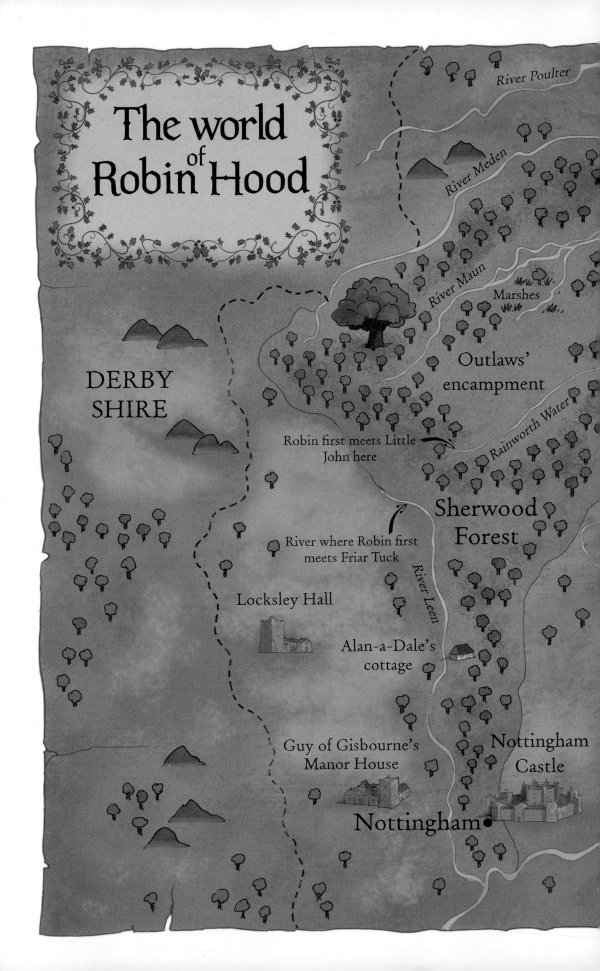

The world of Robin Hood

River Poulter

River Meden

River Maun

Marshes

Outlaws' encampment

DERBY SHIRE

Robin first meets Little John here

Rainworth Water

Sherwood Forest

River where Robin first meets Friar Tuck

River Leen

Locksley Hall

Alan-a-Dale's cottage

Guy of Gisbourne's Manor House

Nottingham Castle

Nottingham

NOTTINGHAM
SHIRE

LINCOLN
SHIRE

River Greet

Arlingford Castle

Dover Beck

River Trent

Scale

0   10 km

6 miles

SCOTLAND

IRELAND

WALES

ENGLAND

Nottingham

England, 1194

With King Richard I away fighting wars in the Holy Land of the Eastern Mediterranean, the country is under the control of his power-hungry brother, Prince John.

Under orders from the Prince, the crooked Sheriff of Nottingham regularly storms through local towns and villages, demanding money from those who can least afford it.

And today is no exception...

GATHER AROUND, PEASANTS!

LISTEN TO THE SHERIFF!

OVER THE WEEKS THAT FOLLOW, THE MYSTERIOUS 'ROBIN HOOD' STRIKES TIME AFTER TIME....

SOON THE SHERIFF OF NOTTINGHAM IS AT HIS WITS' END...

THIS ROBIN HOOD IS MAKING A **FOOL** OF ME! I WANT HIM **FOUND** AND **KILLED**.

I'VE HEARD THAT A LOCAL MILLER HAS HAD DEALINGS WITH HIM.

THEN LET US **ACT!**

SO THAT AFTERNOON, ON THE OUTSKIRTS OF SHERWOOD FOREST...

YOU THERE, MILLER! I HEAR YOU KNOW THE OUTLAW ROBIN HOOD?

WE ALL KNOW OF ROBIN HOOD IN THESE PARTS. BUT HE'S NO OUTLAW.

HA! WHAT ELSE DO YOU CALL A ROGUE WHO ROBS LOYAL SUBJECTS?

HE GIVES IT ALL TO THE POOR. AND HE ONLY TAKES FROM THOSE WHO CAN AFFORD IT.

YES, SON, FROM RICH MEN LIKE PRINCE JOHN'S TAX COLLECTORS.

YOU WILL BE SAFE HERE, LAD. **ROBIN HOOD** HIMSELF WILL LOOK AFTER YOU.

SO, LOCKSLEY **IS** IN LEAGUE WITH ROBIN HOOD.

I'LL SEE TO IT THAT LOCKSLEY'S WEDDING DAY IS **A MEMORABLE ONE.**

AND WITH HIM OUT OF THE WAY, MARIAN CAN BE **MINE!**

GOOD DAY, FATHER!
I WISH TO **CROSS** THE RIVER.

I SHALL BE WITH YOU
PRESENTLY, MY SON.

THE MONK ROWS
OVER TO ROBIN...

AND FERRIES HIM
ACROSS THE RIVER.

BUT THEN...

I'VE CHANGED MY MIND.
PLEASE ROW ME BACK.

AND SO...

SIGH.

BUT THEN...

I'VE CHANGED MY MIND
AGAIN. I SHALL CROSS
AFTER ALL!

42

MARIAN'S FATHER TREATS HIS GUEST TO A FINE DINNER...

AS I SAY, MY LORD, SHE IS **CONFINED** IN HER ROOM UNTIL SHE LEARNS TO **OBEY** HER FATHER.

THANK YOU FOR YOUR **HOSPITALITY**, LORD FITZWALTER. IT'S A PITY YOUR **DAUGHTER** WASN'T ABLE TO JOIN US.

PERHAPS I COULD MAKE HER **SEE SENSE?**

I WOULD BE MOST **GRATEFUL**, MY LORD.

AND SO...

LISTEN TO THE **BISHOP**, MARIAN.

IF WE MIGHT BE **ALONE**, LORD FITZWALTER?

MARIAN RAISES THE PORTCULLIS AND THE PAIR MAKE THEIR ESCAPE...

AND SOON...

WEEKS PASS WITHOUT INCIDENT, UNTIL ONE DAY...

LOOK, ROBIN!

Nottingham Goose Fair

Archery Contest
- open to all
A silver arrow to
the best bowman

HMM. I COULD USE A **CHALLENGE**.

YOU **CAN'T** BE SERIOUS! THE **SHERIFF HIMSELF** IS TO JUDGE THE CONTEST.

YOU'D BE **ARRESTED** ON SIGHT!

I **CAN'T** MISS THIS CHANCE TO TAKE A **PRIZE** FROM THE SHERIFF. I'LL **DISGUISE** MYSELF AS AN **OLD CRUSADER**, BACK FROM THE HOLY LAND.

I KNOW THEIR **STYLE** WELL ENOUGH. YOU RECALL WE SAW **KING RICHARD** HIMSELF LEAD OFF HIS **CRUSADING ARMY**, WILL?

IF YOU **INSIST** ON GOING, LITTLE JOHN AND I WILL **KEEP WATCH** FROM THE CROWD.

THE TRIO PUSH THEIR MOUNTS TO THE LIMIT, BUT...

THEY'RE **GAINING** ON US!

HEAD FOR THE **RIVER!**

NOW WHAT?

TIME TO SAY **GOODBYE** TO YOUR **MOUNT**...

MINUTES LATER, LITTLE JOHN RETURNS...

BUT WHILE HE TAKES THE HORSES TO THE YARD AT THE REAR...

CRUNCH!

WHAT WAS THAT **NOISE** OUTSIDE?

LITTLE JOHN?

NO. IT CAME FROM THE **FRONT** OF THE COTTAGE.

LITTLE JOHN MUST HAVE BEEN **FOLLOWED.**

THE NEXT MOMENT...

THUD!
THUD!
THUD!

SUDDENLY, A FIGURE APPEARS THROUGH THE SMOKE...

WHO ON EARTH...?

STAND FIRM, YOU FOOLS!

THE SMOKE CAUSES ROBIN TO PASS OUT, BUT THE MYSTERIOUS KNIGHT CARRIES HIM AWAY TO SAFETY...

A FEW HOURS LATER, ROBIN IS PROVED CORRECT...

THEY'RE **BACK!** ON **FOOT** THIS TIME, EXCEPT GISBOURNE.

JUST AS I FEARED.

TO ARMS!

FIRE!

WHIZzzz!

WHIZzzz!

WHIZzzz!

BUT GISBOURNE'S MEN RECALL THE KNIGHT FROM THE PREVIOUS EVENING...

HE WALKED THROUGH **FIRE**!

HE'S NOT **HUMAN**!

RUN FOR YOUR LIVES!

WHILE GISBOURNE'S MEN PANIC, THE OUTLAWS TAKE CONTROL...

PUT OUT THE FIRES!

REGROUP!

The story of Robin Hood

The daring, adventurous figure of Robin Hood has enthralled and entertained people of all ages for over 600 years. But where did his story begin, and did such a man really exist?

Medieval minstrels

The earliest known reference to the character is in an English poem called *Piers Plowman* written in the late 14th century. But Robin Hood truly comes into his own in the English ballads of the late 15th and early 16th centuries. Ballads were stories designed to be sung, and were made popular by wandering minstrels who performed them at inns, markets and noblemen's halls.

The earliest surviving ballad referring to Robin Hood is called *Robin and the Monk,* and it features the city of Nottingham as well as Robin's rivalry with the Sheriff.

Alongside Robin and the Sheriff of Nottingham, Guy of Gisbourne, Little John, Much and Will Scarlet all make their first appearances in these early ballads. Maid Marian and Friar Tuck weren't introduced until later.

Robin is described as a yeoman, which was somewhere between a peasant and a knight in status. It wasn't until two plays written in the late 16th century that he was presented as a former nobleman, with the title Earl of Huntingdon. Also around that time came the first mention of Robin robbing from the rich to give to the poor.

From the days of the early ballads, Robin Hood has been associated with two different regions: Sherwood Forest in Nottinghamshire and Barnsdale in Yorkshire.

Robin and the Monk features Sherwood Forest, while another early ballad, *A Gest of Robyn Hode,* mentions both Nottingham and Barnsdale.

It is written in a style closer to that of Yorkshire than Nottinghamshire. Some people have argued that this suggests the tales originated in the northern county.

Barnsdale and Sherwood

However, Barnsdale is only one day's ride from the north of Sherwood Forest, so it's possible that one band of outlaws could have been active in both areas.

May Day games

The legend of Robin Hood also became popular through games that were played as part of medieval May Day festivals. During these games, festivalgoers would dress up as Robin or one of his associates.

A Gest of Robyn Hode is one of the earliest existing printed versions of the legend. After printing became widespread in the late 15th century, Robin appeared in something called a broadside ballad. A broadside was a single sheet of cheap paper printed on one side with a ballad, rhyme or news, often decorated with woodcut illustrations.

Alan-a-Dale first appeared in one such broadside ballad in the 17th century. The ballads were later collected into garlands, a name for cheaply printed books designed to be bought by the poor.

Robin Hood was also mentioned by the playwright William Shakespeare in several of his plays, including *The Two Gentlemen of Verona* and *As You Like It*.

In 1795, the writer Joseph Ritson published a collection of ballads which included a biography of Robin Hood. According to Ritson, Robin Hood was born around 1160 in the Nottinghamshire village of Locksley, and his real name was Robert Fitzooth.

In 1883, American author Robert Pyle wrote *The Merry Adventures of Robin Hood*, one of the first retellings aimed specifically at children. Many subsequent adaptations of the legend took inspiration from this version.

With the invention of radio, film and television, Robin Hood was brought to new generations. *The Adventures of Robin Hood* (1938) and *Robin Hood: Prince of Thieves* (1991) are two of the most famous movie versions of the legend. His best-known appearances on television include *The Adventures of Robin Hood* (1955-59), *Robin of Sherwood* (1984-86) and *Robin Hood* (2006-09).

Some experts believe that although Robin Hood is now largely known as a fictional character, the stories are based on a real person. But exactly who that person was will probably never be discovered. Variations on the name Robin Hood were fairly common in medieval England. From 1261 onwards it appears on several lists of criminals across England, from Berkshire in the south to Yorkshire in the north.

Robin Hood

Robin Hood may have even been a standard alias used by thieves. So if the famous outlaw did exist, his real name will almost certainly remain unknown.

But whether he was a real person or not, the name of Robin Hood has become so well-loved all over the world that the man and his adventures will never die.

Russell Punter was born in Bedfordshire, England. From an early age he enjoyed writing and illustrating his own stories. He trained as a graphic designer at art college in West Sussex before entering publishing in 1987. He has written over fifty books for children, ranging from original rhyming stories to adaptations of classic novels.

Matteo Pincelli was born in Bergamo, Italy. He studied anatomy and comics drawing in Bologna and later formed an animation studio together with eight colleagues. He has also worked in France with a production company based in Paris, and has lived in Berlin, Germany, and Milan, Italy. Today he is based in Fano in the Marche region of Italy, where he occupies himself mainly with work as a storyboard artist, television cartoonist and illustrator of children's books.

Mike Collins has been creating comics for over 25 years. Starting on *Spider-Man* and *Transformers* for Marvel UK, he has also worked for DC, 2000AD and a host of other publishers. In that time he's written or drawn almost all the major characters for each company – *Wonder Woman, Batman, Superman, Flash, Teen Titans, X-Men, Captain Britain, Judge Dredd, Sláine, Rogue Trooper, Darkstars, Peter Cannon: Thunderbolt* and more. He currently draws a series of noir crime fiction graphic novels, *Varg Veum*, in Norse. He also provides storyboards for TV and films, including *Doctor Who, Sherlock, Igam Ogam, Claude, Hana's Helpline* and *Horrid Henry*.

Cover design: Matt Preston

First published in 2017 by Usborne Publishing Ltd., Usborne House,
83-85 Saffron Hill, London EC1N 8RT, England. www.usborne.com
Copyright © 2017 Usborne Publishing Ltd.